Amazing Animals

Ron Benson
Lynn Bryan
Kim Newlove
Liz Stenson
Iris Zammit

CONSULTANTS
Lillian Blakey
Florence Brown
Estella Clayton
Kathryn D'Angelo
Susan Elliott-Johns
Charolette Player
Shari Schwartz
Lynn Swanson
Helen Tomassini
Debbie Toope

Prentice Hall Ginn

Contents

Rabbits   3
article from *Click* magazine

The Tiny Patient   10
picture book story
by Judy Pedersen

True or False?   17
factual recount
by Nancy Davidson

Kangaroo Up a Tree   24
report by Annie Sutton

Brontosaurus   30
poem by Gail Kredenser

Katie and Sankeerth's Writing
diagram

Rabbits

from Click *magazine*

These rabbits have just been born.
A newborn rabbit has no fur.
It cannot see or hear,
but it has a good sense of smell.

This is the mother rabbit.
The baby rabbits drink
the mother's milk for food.
The mother made the nest
before her babies were born
and lined it with dried grass, moss,
and fur from her own body.
She leaves her babies alone in the nest
when she is not giving them milk.

When a rabbit is one week old,
its fur is starting to grow.
The baby rabbit will soon be crawling
around in the nest and opening its eyes.

When the rabbit is
two weeks old,
it can see and hear.
It still drinks
its mother's milk for food.
Can you see that its soft fur
is getting longer and thicker?

Three weeks after being born,
the rabbit is still very small. But already
it is old enough to explore and play
in the grass and leaves near its nest.

These rabbits are about four weeks old. Can you see that their ears are getting longer? The rabbits play together outside the nest, and huddle close together to keep warm. The mother rabbit and father rabbit stay near and warn the babies of any danger.

When the rabbit is five weeks old, it no longer needs its mother's milk. It eats seeds, grasses, roots, and vegetables instead. Rabbits need to chew hard food like carrots to keep their teeth from growing too long.

The young rabbit is now six weeks old.
It is still not as big as its mother,
but it has grown up a lot.
And in just a few more months, the rabbit
will be ready to have babies of its own.

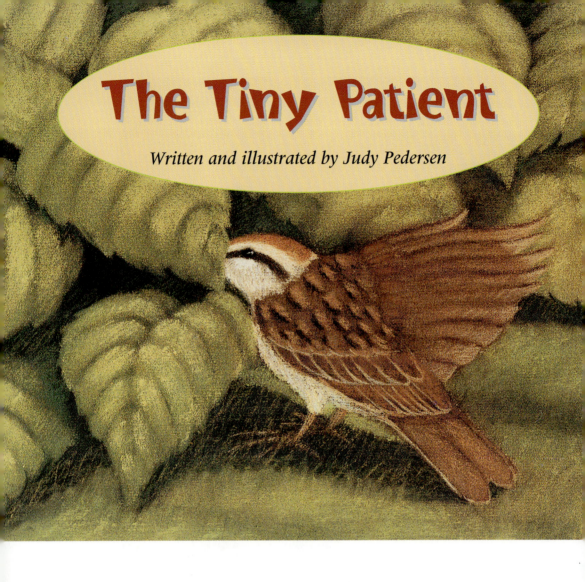

The Tiny Patient

Written and illustrated by Judy Pedersen

One day my grandmother and I
heard some whispering leaves
and a low-pitched *tseep*.
Under the eaves, behind a bush,
we found a little chipping sparrow.
She was brown and grey
and had a broken wing.

Through the dewy grass we inched our way
closer and closer to her soft, quivering body.
She was very frightened and looked to be
in pain as she held that wing stiffly at her side.

My grandmother didn't know anything
about taking care of wild chipping sparrows,
but she said, "The poor thing must be hungry,"
and suggested a bun and some water.
We covered her carefully
with my grandmother's handkerchief
and brought her into our warm, safe kitchen.

Nibble, nibble, nibble.
The bun became breadcrumbs.
Dribble, dribble, dribble.
The water became a cool drink.
In the warmth of our kitchen
a tiny heart throbbed,
tip, tap, tip, tap, tip, tap.

Outside our window
the morning birds kept watch.
"Let's make a nest for her!"
My grandmother agreed.
So we took some white, white cotton
and made a bird-size sickbed.

We found her a sunny spot
by the window so she could look out
and feel close to her friends and the trees.
And every day, we fed her
soft buns and water,
until her wing had mended
and she was strong again.

Then, one summer day,
she was well enough to fly,
so up, up, up, she went—
goodbye!

True or False?

by Nancy Davidson
Illustrated by Bo-Kim Louie

Last week I heard my dad say, "Bats are blind," and I asked myself, "Is that true?" So I looked in my big book about animals and I discovered . . .

. . . it wasn't true.
Bats can see. They look like they're blind
because they fly around in a zig-zag way.
They do this to catch small flying insects
in mid-air. Bats can hear very well,
so they also find their food in the dark
by listening for the sounds of the insects.

A month ago when we got our new cat,
my brother told me that cats have nine lives.
I said to myself, "I think that's only a story."
So I asked my mom and she said . . .

. . . it was false.
She explained that long ago in Egypt,
people thought cats were gods
and had many lives. But cats, like people,
have only one life. They live
about fifteen years or more.
Cats are so clever and quick
that they can jump from high places,
and usually land safely without getting hurt.
That's why people say cats have many lives.

On the weekend
when my cousin came over,
he said he read in a book
that bees die soon after
they sting you.
"Is that true or false?"
I wondered.
My cousin is usually right,
but I checked
on the Internet anyway,
and I discovered . . .

. . . it was true.
Most bees can sting only once.
They use their stingers, which have hooks called barbs.
When a bee stings, the barbs stick in the skin and then the stinger breaks off.
Once a bee loses its stinger, it dies.
Queen bees can sting many times because their stingers don't have any barbs.

Yesterday when I came home from school,
I told my family that fish can climb trees.
Everyone said, "That's not true!"
I answered, "Yes it is. We watched a video
in school today, and we learned that . . .

. . . tiny fish called mud skippers can climb.
They crawl onto tree branches that bend
over into the water. Mud skippers
can breathe in air as well as in water."
Guess what my family is doing now? They're
looking up *mud skipper* in the encyclopedia!

Kangaroo Up a Tree

by Annie Sutton

You have heard about kangaroos that hop along the ground. But have you heard of kangaroos that live in trees most of the time? They even sleep in the treetops.

Great Climbers and Jumpers

When it wants to climb a tree, the kangaroo first jumps up and wraps its arms around the tree trunk. Then it climbs up by sliding its arms and hopping with its feet. When it is ready to come down, it climbs down tail first.

Matschie's Tree Kangaroo

It can jump three metres from one tree across to the next. It can also jump as far as nine metres down from one tree to another.

- 50–75 cm tall
- mass of 10–13 kg

Appearance

- long tail to help it balance while climbing

- thick fur to help it keep dry and warm in the rain

- large back feet with pads of rough skin to keep it from slipping on branches

Food
- leaves
- vines
- ferns
- wild fruit
- grass
- bark
- nuts
- flowers
- mosses

- large, strong nails to help it grab branches

Habitat
- mountain rainforests in Papua New Guinea and Australia

Papua New Guinea

Australia

27

Tree Kangaroo Babies

A tree kangaroo baby is called a *joey*. When it's born, the joey is about the size of a thumb. The baby climbs into its mother's pouch to drink her milk and sleep.

Around $5\frac{1}{2}$ months, it looks out of the pouch. Around $7\frac{1}{2}$ months, it comes out of the pouch to explore. It learns to climb on small branches. At 10 months, it leaves the pouch for short spells. Around $1\frac{1}{2}$ years, the joey leaves its mother and learns to find its own food.

Endangered Creature!

Today tree kangaroos are endangered. Hunters kill them for their meat and fur. Other people destroy their homes when they cut down the trees.

Scientists are working hard to make sure that tree kangaroos survive.

Perhaps one day you will visit a place where tree kangaroos live, or see them in a zoo.

Brontosaurus

by Gail Kredenser
Illustrated by Laurie Stein

The giant brontosaurus
Was a prehistoric chap
With four fat feet to stand on
And a very skimpy lap.
The scientists assure us
Of a most amazing thing—
A brontosaurus blossomed
When he had a chance to sing !

(The bigger brontosauruses,
Who liked to sing in choruses,
Would close their eyes
and harmonize
And sing most anything.)

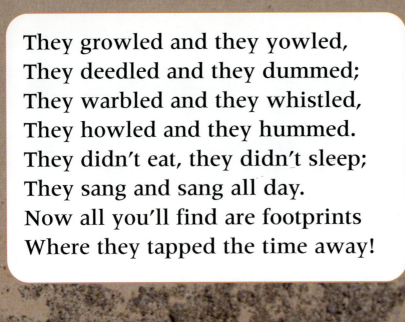

They growled and they yowled,
They deedled and they dummed;
They warbled and they whistled,
They howled and they hummed.
They didn't eat, they didn't sleep;
They sang and sang all day.
Now all you'll find are footprints
Where they tapped the time away!